a walk through the
Winter Woods

Written by Colleen Monroe

Illustrated by Michael Glenn Monroe

One winter morning I looked outside,

and what I saw was such a surprise.

Jack Frost had come to my window at night,

and the glass panes shimmered

in the first morning light.

As I peeked outside my eyes did see,
the new fallen snow on every tree.

Mounds of white crystals covered the land,
and I knew that a walk through the woods was at hand.

As I dressed myself to go outside,
my trusty companion by my side,

I wondered what Mother Nature had in store,
outside in the snow just beyond my door.

As I go walking through the winter wood,
animals hide as I knew they would.

Hiding in the brush and in the tree,
I can't see them but they can see me.

Through the winter wood as I go walking,
all around me the birds are talking.

I wonder what they are trying to say,
as through the branches they hop and play.

Farther into the woods I slowly go,
the path is now covered with deeper snow.

My furry companion breaks the trail for me,
anxious to see what's behind every tree.

Pine branches dipping, heavy with snow,
give the small bunny a place to go.

Tucked in and warm in his icy house,
he watches us pass, silent as a mouse.

The crunching of snow beneath my boot,
startles an owl who gives a soft hoot.

With the whisper of wings he slowly takes flight,
silently soaring just out of my sight.

A little red squirrel runs across our trail,
acknowledging us with a flick of his tail.

Trying to remember his hiding places,
but the mountains of snow have covered the traces.

Trying to tread lightly I continue my walk,
quietly being watched by a red-tailed hawk.

Surveying his domain from high in the tree,
not to be bothered by a wanderer like me.

As I go walking through the winter wood,
snowflakes fall and stick to my hood.

Shimmering and dancing they make not a sound,
whirling and twirling they fall to the ground.

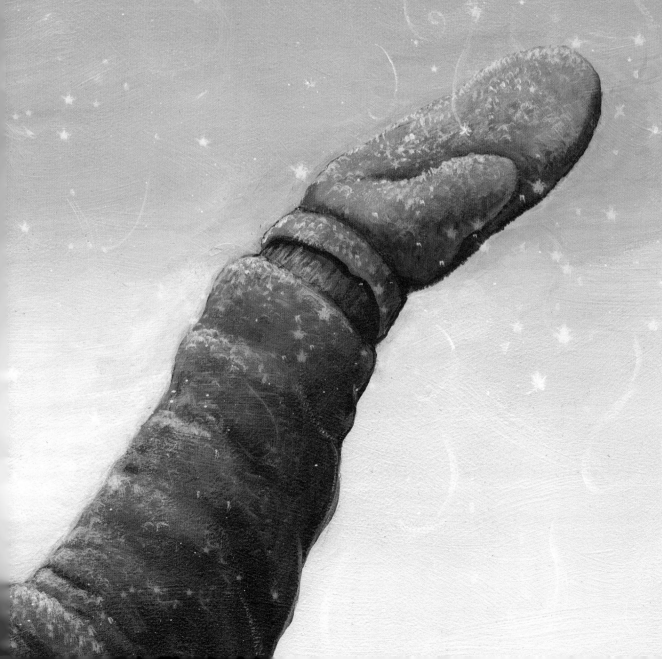

Moving along farther, steady and slow,
we happened upon a bedded down doe.

She watches us keenly with her soft brown eyes,
silently hoping that we just walk by.

The woods after a snowfall are silent and deep,
like everything there has fallen asleep.

We quietly continue, not making a sound,
Our footsteps are muffled by the snow on the ground.

As I go walking through the winter wood,
I know I'm not dressed as warm as I should.

Cold winds blow and scratch my face,
I wish I was home by the warm fireplace.

My boots grow heavy as I start to turn back,
fresh fallen snow has covered my track.

The footprints I made I can no longer see,
the snow has erased any evidence of me.